# A Plastic World

Alan Trussell-Cullen

Australia • Brazil • Japan • Korea • Mexico • Singapore • Spain • United Kingdom • United States

A Plastic World

Fast Forward
Blue Level 11

Text: Alan Trussell-Cullen
Editor: Kate McGough
Design: James Lowe
Series design: James Lowe
Production controller: Emma Hayes
Photo research: Corrina Tauschke
Audio recordings: Juliet Hill, Picture Start
Spoken by: Matthew King and Abbe Holmes
Reprint: Siew Han Ong

Acknowledgements
The author and publisher would like to acknowledge permission to reproduce material from the following sources: Photographs by ANT Photo Library/Frank Park, p 13 top; istockphoto.com, back cover top right, p 10/ Branislava Becejsk, p 4 top/ Chris Bishop, p 12 bottom/ Mark Evans, cover inset, p 9 right/ Melissa King, p 4 bottom/ Jonah Manning, p 12 top/ Nancy Louie, p 4 centre left; Lindsay Edwards, back cover, pp 3, 5 bottom, 6-7, 8, 9 top, 9 centre left, 9 bottom left, 15; Michelle Cottrill, pp 14-15; Newsphotos.com.au/Carmelo Bazzano, p 11; Photolibrary.com/ Imagesource, p 11 bottom/ Colin Monteath, p 14/ Science Photo library, p 13 bottom; Photos.com, p 6 bottom left; Science Museum Pictorial/Science & Society Picture Library, p 5 top left.



ISBN 978 0 17 012556 7
ISBN 978 0 17 012549 9 (set)

Cengage Learning Australia
Level 7, 80 Dorcas Street
South Melbourne, Victoria Australia 3205
Phone: 1300 790 853

Cengage Learning New Zealand
Unit 4B Rosedale Office Park
331 Rosedale Road, Albany, North Shore NZ 0632
Phone: 0508 635 766

For learning solutions, visit cengage.com.au

Printed in Australia by Ligare Pty Ltd
8 9 10 11 12 13 20 19 18 17 16

THE UNIVERSITY OF
MELBOURNE

Evaluated in independent research by staff from the Department of Language, Literacy and Arts Education at the University of Melbourne.

# A Plastic World

Alan Trussell-Cullen

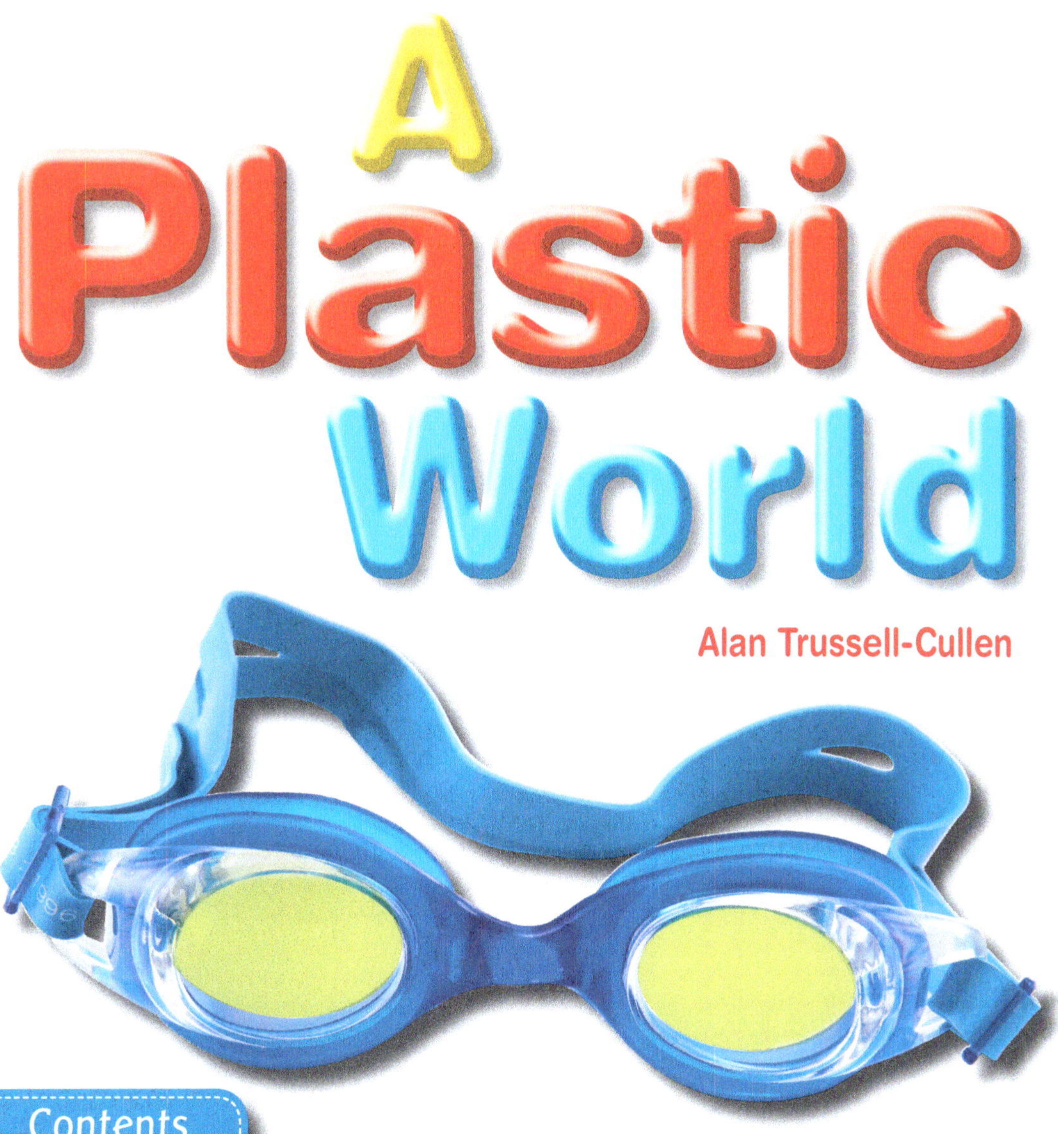

## Contents

# A Plastic World

For years, people made things they needed from **materials** they found in the world around them. Two of these materials were wood and metal.

In 1862, Alexander Parkes **invented** plastic, and the world began to change.

Today, all kinds of things are made of plastic.

Plastic has changed the world and how people live. Just about everything in our homes is made of plastic or has some plastic parts.

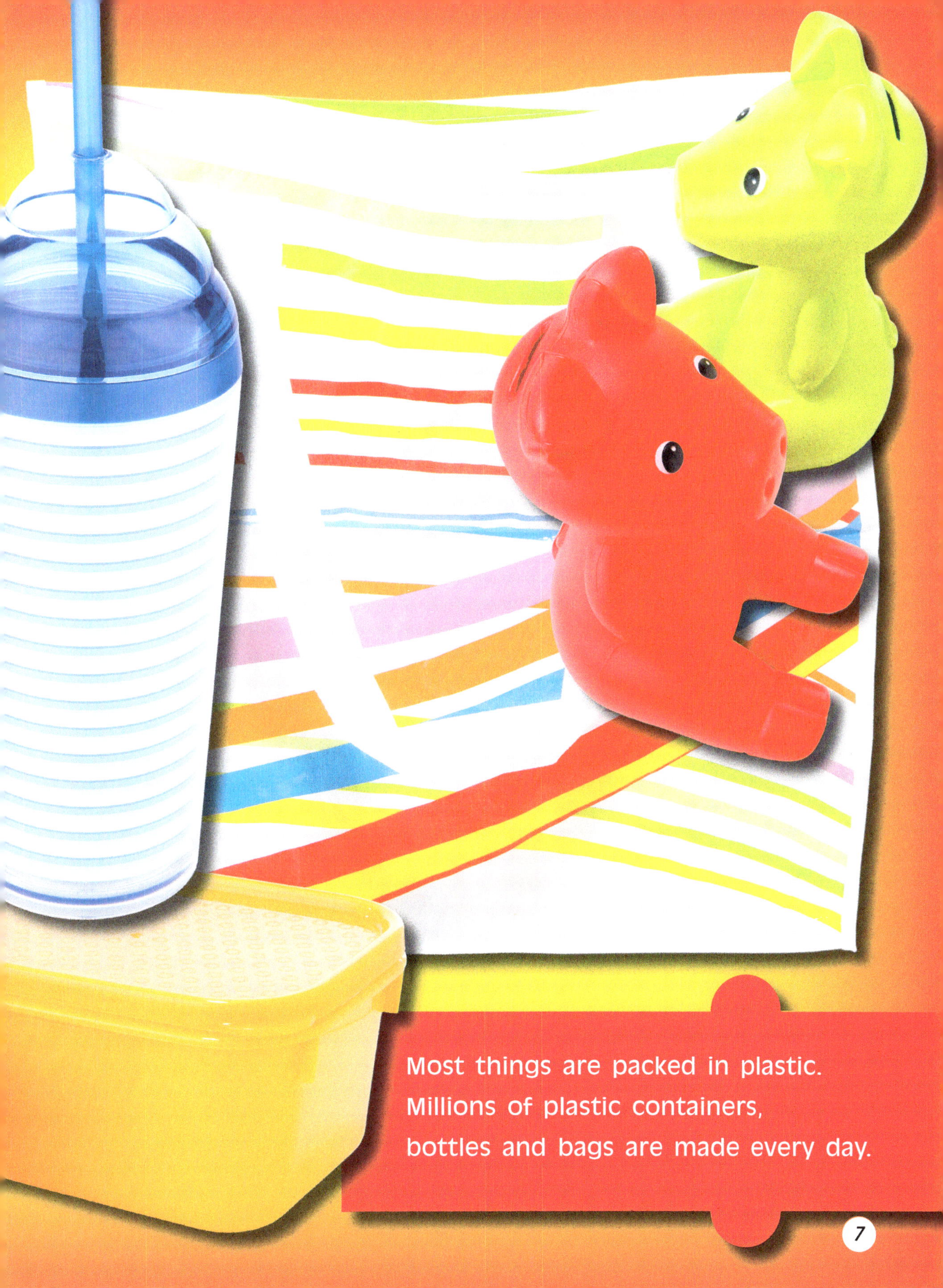

Most things are packed in plastic. Millions of plastic containers, bottles and bags are made every day.

# Chapter 2

# Is Plastic Good or Bad?

Some people think plastic has been good for the world. Some people think it has been bad.

## Good Things about Plastic

First, plastic is cheap, so lots of things made from plastic are cheap.

*Running Words 151*

Secondly, plastic is light.
Plastics are used in most toys.
Plastics can be made hard or soft, and can be made into different shapes.
Lots of toys made from plastic are both light and cheap.

# Bad Things about Plastic

First, when plastic is being made, it sends gases into the air. These gases can be bad for people and the environment.

Secondly, plastic bags are bad for the environment.
When plastic bags become rubbish,
a lot of them end up in one place.
The bags stop air and water from getting into the soil.
Plants that grow in the soil die.

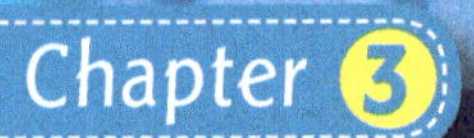


# Plastic as Rubbish

Plastic is good for packing things, but too much of it ends up as rubbish. This is a big problem for the environment.

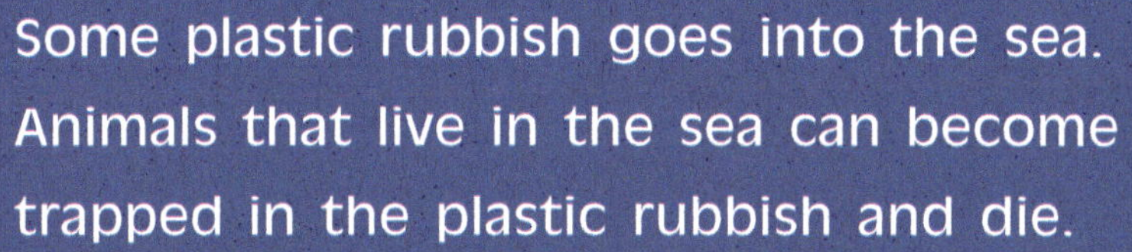

Some plastic rubbish goes into the sea. Animals that live in the sea can become trapped in the plastic rubbish and die.

Another terrible thing about plastic is that a lot of it ends up in **landfills**. People have so much rubbish now that the world is running out of land for landfills.

# Recycle!

Plastic can be good and bad for the world.
Plastic helps people in lots of ways,
but it can also be bad for the environment.
People need to look at what they do with plastic
so that they keep the environment safe.

There are a number of things people can do to stop
so much plastic going into rubbish.

**Recycle** plastic so it gets made into something else.

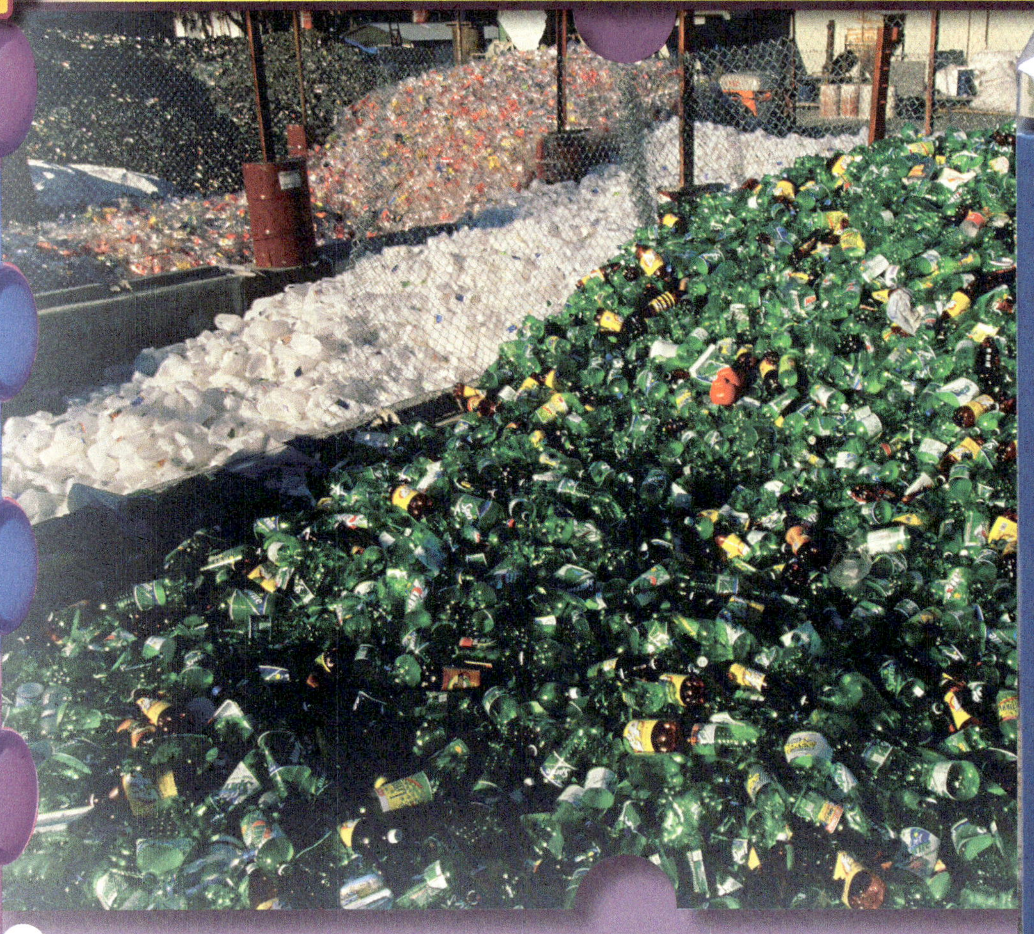

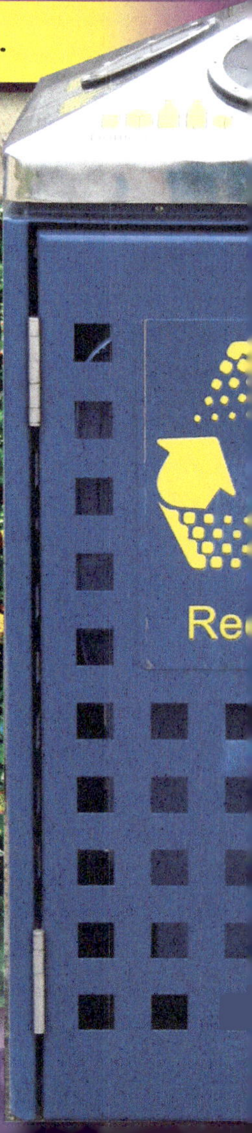

Find different ways to use plastic.

## Glossary

**invented** thought up the idea for something, or created it for the first time

**landfills** places where rubbish is dumped

**materials** substances that things are made from

**recycle** to use something again, for something else

## Index